Bernard Francis Moore

Captain Jack or the Irish Outlaw

An Original Irish Drama in Three Acts

Bernard Francis Moore

Captain Jack or the Irish Outlaw
An Original Irish Drama in Three Acts

ISBN/EAN: 9783744736312

Printed in Europe, USA, Canada, Australia, Japan

Cover: Foto ©Andreas Hilbeck / pixelio.de

More available books at **www.hansebooks.com**

OR

HE IRISH OUTLAW

An Original Irish Drama in Three Acts

BY

BERNARD F. MOORE

—————

BOSTON

1894

CHARACTERS.

CAPTAIN EDWARD GORDON, *commanding a detachment of Her Majesty's soldiers in Ireland.*

SQUIRE SHANNON, *whose love for Aline blinds him to all sense of right.*

JOHN DRISCOLL, *the Rebel leader, known as Captain Jack.*

BARNEY DONOVAN, *a sprig of the old sod.*

TEDDY BURKE, *the informer, in the pay of Shannon.*

TIM BURNS, *a half-witted lad.*

LIEUTENANT ROGERS, *of Her Majesty's soldiers.*

ALINE DRISCOLL, *sister of John, and in love with the Captain.*

NELLIE SHANNON, *the Squire's daughter.*

KATE KELLEY, *a true-hearted colleen.*

MARY, *a servant at the Squire's.*

ACT FIRST. — Home of the Driscolls. Morning. The Arrest.

ACT SECOND. — The Squire's Study. Night. The Escape.

ACT THIRD. — Home of the Driscolls. Next morning. The pardon.

COSTUMES.

(IRISH, 1867.)

CAPTAIN GORDON. — *Act First.* — Uniform of British officer, — red coat and waistcoat, white breeches, black riding-boots, three-cornered hat, sword and belt. *Act Second.* — Black coat and pants, coat is short and buttoned tight, black riding-boots with spurs, and black slouched hat. *Act Third.* — Same.

SQUIRE SHANNON. — *Act First.* — Black satin coat and knee-breeches, black silk stockings, low-cut buckled shoes, black hat, long brown coat with cape, and gold-headed cane. *Act Second.* — Dark blue smoking-jacket, cap, and slippers. *Act Third.* — Same as Act First.

JOHN DRISCOLL. — *Act First.* — Gray coat and breeches. black riding-boots, black hat, a long black coat with cape. *Acts Second and Third.* — Same.

BARNEY DONOVAN. — *Act First.* — Gray corduroy breeches. gray coat with wide lappels, white shirt with large collar and open at neck, light blue stockings, low-cut buckled shoes, and small gray felt hat. *Acts Second and Third.* — Same.

TEDDY BURKE. — *Act First.* — Face very dirty and repulsive, black wig, bald, tattered black coat buttoned to the chin, black knee-breeches and stockings, low-cut shoes, and battered high hat. *Acts Second and Third.* — Same.

TIM BURNS. — Tattered coat and knee-breeches, gray stockings, low-cut shoes, and soft hat.

LIEUTENANT ROGERS. — Uniform of an English officer.

ALINE DRISCOLL. — *Act First.* — Neat black dress. *Act Second.* — Light gray dress, black cloak and hood lined with red. *Act Third.* — White muslin dress, with a pink ribbon tied in a bow around neck.

NELLIE SHANNON. — *Act First.* — Fashionable walking-dress of black velvet, hat and gloves to match dress. *Act Second.* — Black dress, with white collar and cuffs. *Act Third.* — Same as Act First.

KATE KELLEY. — Dark green colored bodice, red petticoat, black stockings and slippers.

MARY. — Dark colored dress.

ACTS FIRST AND THIRD.

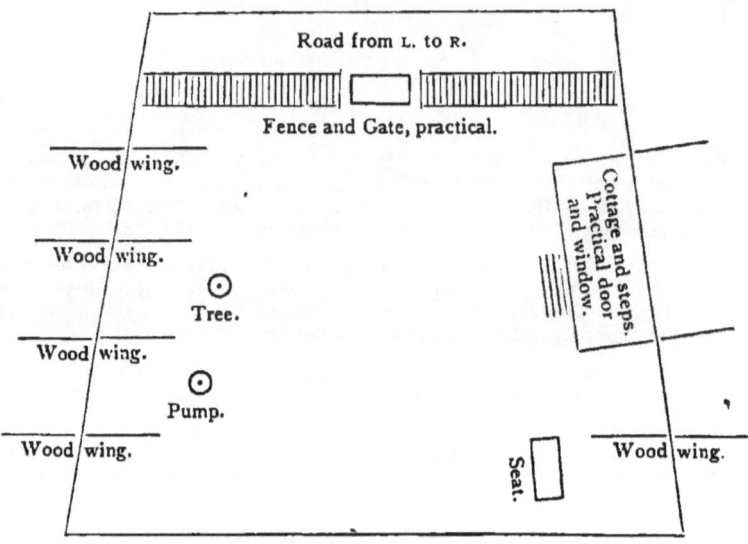

SCENE. — Set cottage, L. 2 and 3 E. Pump, trough, and dipper, R. 2 E. Tree, R. 3 E. White picket-fence running from L. to R.; in the centre of fence a gate to open in; road runs from L. to R., outside of fence.

ACT SECOND.

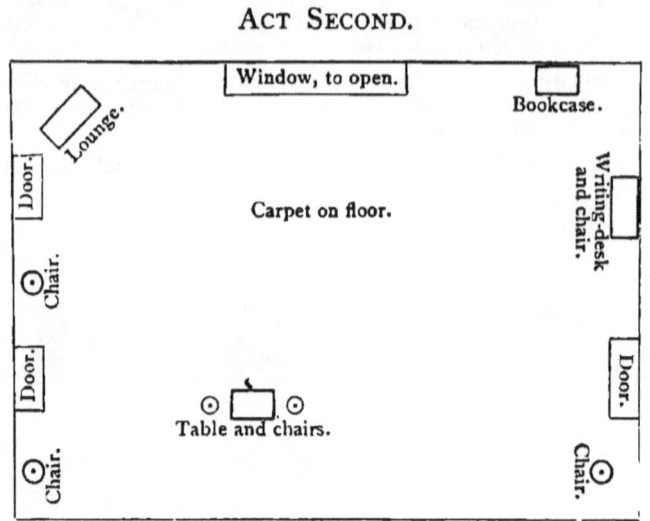

SCENE. — A room; square-doors L. H. and R. 2 E., and R. 4 E. Writing-desk and chair, L. 4 E; Bookcase, L. C. Lounge, R. C. Large window, C., to open. Carpet on floor. Table and chairs, R. 2 E.; other chairs around room.

CAPTAIN JACK.

ACT I.

SCENE. — *Set cottage,* L. 2. E. ; *pump,* R. 2. E. ; *tree,* R. 3. E. ; *fence at back,* 4. E. ; *road running from* L. *to* R. ; *gate in* C. *of fence. Music, " Girl I left behind me," at rise of curtain.*

ALINE (*at pump ; looking off* R.). I wonder who this strange young man coming down the road can be. A soldier from the looks of his clothes. (*Suddenly.*) Mercy on me, he's coming here ! (*Quickly.*) I know what I'll do. I'll pretend I don't see him, and find out who he is and what he wants in coming here. (*Begins to pump, and sings.*)

> " I'm lonesome since I crossed the hills,
> And o'er the moor that's sedgy ;
> With heavy thoughts my mind is filled,
> Since I have parted with Peggy.
> Whene'er I turn to view the place,
> The tears do fall and blind me,
> When I think of the charming grace,
> Of the girl I left behind me."

(CAPTAIN GORDON *enters from* R. *and stands listening attentively at gate,* C.)

CAPTAIN GORDON (*at end of verse applauds*). Bravo ! bravo ! Charming, young woman, I assure you. Allow me (*enters gate* C.) to congratulate you in possessing such a magnificent voice. You should go to England and study for the operatic stage.

AL. (*aside*). I wonder who can he be. (*Aloud.*) Thank you, sir, you flatter me. (*Bows.*) But I have no desire to visit England just yet. Now, sir, if I'm not too bold, may I ask who you are?

CAP. (*laughing*). Why, certainly. My name is Edward Gordon, commanding a detachment of Her Majesty's soldiers.

AL. (*aside*). My brother's friend ! (*Aloud.*) And what are you doing so far away from the rest of your comrades at the present time, Captain Gordon?

CAP. (*aside*). Charming girl, but devilish inquisitive. (*Aloud.*) Well, to tell you the candid truth, I had a motive in visiting this place to-day.

AL. (*in surprise*). Indeed !

5

CAP. Yes; I am trying to find the home of an old college chum of mine.

AL. And do you require the aid of soldiers to assist you?

CAP. (*hastily*). Oh, no; the soldiers are here to hunt down the rebels of the mountain.

AL. (*excitedly*). What! Hunt down Captain Jack and his men?

CAP. (*quickly*). You know him then?

AL. I have heard of him and his followers. Now what is the name of your friend?

CAP. John Driscoll. You see it's some years since we met last. But I am sure I would know him if I could only meet him. The last letter I received from him, told me he lived in this neighborhood somewhere. But as to the exact locality, I'm at fault.

AL. Then you need go no farther. (*Points around.*) For this is the home of John Driscoll and his ancestors for ages past.

CAP. (*looking around*). Well, I'm glad to know that. Thank Heaven, my journey through the mountains is over for the present. By the way, my dear girl (*looks at pail of water*), that seems to be sparkling water you have there. Would you oblige me with a drink?

AL. (*hands him dipperful*). Here you are, sir.

CAP. (*takes dipper and holds it up*). Thank you. (*Tastes it.*) Ah, how delicious! And how true are the words of the poet. (*Sings.*)

> " How dear to my heart are the scenes of my childhood,
>   When fond recollection presents them to view!
>   The orchard, the meadow, the deep tangled wildwood,
>   And every loved spot which my infancy knew."

AL. (*applauding*). Bravo !

CAP. (*drinks. and hands her back dipper*). And now, seeing you know who I am, would you have the kindness to inform me who you are?

AL. (*aside*). I'll play a joke on the captain. (*Aloud.*) My name is Kate Kelley, sir.

CAP. A very pretty name, I assure you. Do you live with the Driscolls?

AL. Yes, sir; I am Miss Aline's maid.

CAP. (*aside*). Only a servant, and so handsome. (*Aloud.*) Kate, I have heard Miss Aline is a very beautiful girl?

AL. (*aside*). He don't suspect who I am. (*Aloud.*) So the people all say, sir.

CAP. Kate, do you know you are very pretty?

AL. (*aside*). Thank you for the compliment. (*Aloud.*) You do me proud, sir.

CAP. Yes, my dear girl, you are indeed very beautiful. And the name of Kate Kelley well becomes such a charming creature as you are.

AL. Well, you might like the name of Kelley, but I don't. And what's more, I am going to change it as soon as possible.

Cap. (*laughing*). Ah, you have a lover then, you sly little fox?

Al. (*in surprise*). Of course I have or how do you think I could change it? Do you think I want to die an old maid? (*Pouting.*) For shame, sir, to hurt a poor girl's feelings by such base insinuations.

Cap. (*humbly*). Miss Kate, I ask a thousand pardons.

Al. (*laughing*). Oh, one will do just as well.

Cap. (*aside*). By Jove, the more I see of her, the better I like her. (*Aloud.*) Miss Kate, may I inquire the name of your future husband?

Al. (*aside*). Now I'm in for it. (*Aloud.*) Oh, we all call him Barney Donovan.

Cap. (*aside*). Barney, I envy you. (*Aloud.*) I hope Barney Donovan, as you call him, will make you a happy husband.

Al. Barney's all right. He thinks the world of me.

Cap. Fortunate Barney.

Al. (*aside*). The Captain is getting sentimental. (*Aloud.*) Do you think so, sir?

Cap. Indeed I do. (*Hands her piece of money.*) Here, Miss Kate, this will help you and Barney to furnish your future home.

Al. (*taking money*). Thank you, sir. (*Aside.*) I'll keep this as a remembrance of the Captain's first visit to Ireland.

Cap. And, Kate, — you will allow me to call you Kate, — you know it's customary to kiss the bride at the wedding.

Al. (*aside*). I wonder what he means? (*Aloud.*) So I have heard, sir.

Cap. And as I don't think I'll be present at your wedding, I think I'll take mine now, if you don't object.

Al. (*in astonishment*). Is it going to kiss me you are?

Cap. (*laughing*). Well, that is my intention. But if you see fit to object —

Al. (*quickly*). I don't object in the least. But you see, Barney may not like it.

(*Enter* BARNEY *from road*, L.)

Cap. I'll make it all right with Barney.

Barney (*at gate*, C.). I wondher what divilment is Miss Aline up to now.

Al. If you think you can you may take one.

Cap. Oh, I'll settle Barney. (*Kisses her.*)

Bar. Oh, murther, did ye iver see the likes of that?

Al. (*looking around in confusion*). Barney here! (*Exit into house*, L.)

Cap. (*seeing* BARNEY). Barney, you rascal. is it you?

Bar. (*in surprise*). Mr. Gordon!

Cap. (*shaking hands*). Barney, you don't know how glad I am to see you.

Bar. An' so am I, sur. But what are ye doin' in this part of the country?

CAP. Well, I was sent here principally to hunt down the mountain rebels.

BAR. (*slowly*). Huntin' rebels, did ye say, sir?

CAP. Yes, Barney: I am sorry to say such is one of the reasons I am in this part of Ireland to-day.

BAR. An' do ye think ye'll find Captain Jack an' his men?

CAP. Well, I can't just say. I may and I may not. Be that as it may, I don't think I'll break my heart if I don't. In fact, I have a great desire to meet this famous outlaw.

BAR. To make a prisoner of him?

CAP. No, Barney, as a friend, to see what kind of a man he really is. I have heard a great deal about him and his deeds. In fact, his name is the chief topic of conversation in England.

BAR. He is really an' truly a great man. But let me tell ye, Mr. Gordon, he will niver be taken alive, to die on an English scaffold.

CAP. But the fox must sleep, Barney.

BAR. Very thrue, sur. But if he's iver taken alive, it will be through the treachery of friends.

CAP. Let us hope not. (*Warmly.*) Barney, do you know I pity the poor Irish rebels from the bottom of my heart? Poor homeless outcasts! What are they fighting for but their own? You may think this strange, coming as it does from one who wears the uniform of an English soldier, and claims England as the land of his birth. I don't believe in the policy adopted by Great Britain, in the treatment of Ireland and her people.

BAR. (*excitedly*). Good for ye, me brave boy. Captain dear, ye should have been born an Irishman!

CAP. (*fervently*). I wish to God I had.

BAR. Niver fear, Captain, I'll make an Irishman of ye, if ye shtay in Ireland long enough.

CAP. (*laughing*). Thank you, Barney, I haven't the slightest doubt of it. But I had a deeper motive than chasing rebels in coming here to-day.

BAR. (*in surprise*). Indade! (*Aside.*) What the divil does he mane now?

CAP. Yes, Barney, I came to see my old college chum, your master, John Driscoll.

BAR. Thin ye nade go no farther. Shure this is the shpot.

CAP. Yes, so Miss Kate informed me.

BAR. (*in surprise*). Who?

CAP. Why, your sweetheart, Kate Kelley.

BAR. Did she tell ye her name was Kate Kelley?

CAP. (*in surprise*). Why, yes.

BAR. Is it the young lady I saw ye kiss?

CAP. To be sure it is. I gave her a kiss as my wedding gift.

BAR. (*laughing*). Oh, holy mother, will ye listen to that.

CAP. (*in amazement*). What the devil ails you, Barney? Explain before I'm tempted to break your head.

BAR. (*laughing*). In a minute, sor.

CAP. Barney, stop laughing!

BAR. I'm as sober as a judge, sor.

CAP. Now, sir, what is the cause of all this mirth?

BAR. (*earnestly*). Captain Gordon, don't ye really know who it was ye just kissed?

CAP. Why, of course I know. I kissed the girl you're going to make your future wife.

BAR. Not a dom bit of it, sor!

CAP. (*in surprise*). No? Then, in the name of goodness, who was it?

BAR. (*laughing*). John Driscoll's sisther, Aline!

CAP. Oh, the devil!

BAR. Fact, I assure ye.

CAP. (*aside*). I'm more than half in love with the little rogue already. (*Aloud.*) Barney, take me to the young lady, so that I may apologize for my rudeness of manner towards her.

BAR. Come into the house with me an' I'll introduce her to ye. Don't appear bashful, or yer doom is saled. Aline is a perfect witch among bashful men. So be warned in time.

CAP. Lead on, Barney, and I'll follow you. (*Exit into house*, L.)

(*Enter* SQUIRE *and* TEDDY *from road*, R.)

SQUIRE (*entering gate*, C., *and looking around*). And you are positive this is the place you tracked the rebel captain to last night?

TEDDY (*entering gate*, C *and looking around*). I'll shware to it on a shtack of Bibles as high as the mountain, sor.

SQU. Good! Then it's as I suspected all along. Captain Jack the rebel leader and John Driscoll are one and the same person. But, Teddy, we must have proof. To have him arrested without proof of his guilt being found, would never do.

TED. Shure that's an asy matther, Squire.

SQU. (*in surprise*). You don't mean to say you have the necessary proof?

TED. Faith an' I have, Squire.

SQU. Where is it?

TED. Listen a moment to me, sor.

SQU. (*attentively*). I'm all attention.

TED. Lasht night I waited until the meetin' of the rebels was over. Thin I follered the lader to this place. Who he was I did not know, as he was masked. Whin he entered this yard he looked cautiously around to see if he was observed. All seemed quiet. He thin removed the mask, an' I beheld the face of John Driscoll!

SQU. But are you positive he is Captain Jack?

TED. Of course I am. Wasn't I at the meetin'? Didn't I hear him make a speech? An' didn't I hear the rest of them callin' him Captain Jack?

SQU. I believe you. But while Captain Jack, or rather John Driscoll, was removing his mask, where were you?

TED. (*pointing to fence*). Hid behind the fence. Before he wint into the house he hid his mask an' pistols.

SQU. (*excitedly*). And you know where they are concealed?

TED. To be shure I do.

SQU. Where are they?

TED. In the hollow of yonder tree. (*Points to tree*, R. 2 E.)

SQU. See if they are there yet.

TED. (*looks around cautiously*). All right, squire. (*Goes to tree, and from hollow takes black mask and pistols.*) Here they are, sor, safe an' sound. (*Hands them to* SQUIRE.)

SQU. Good! (*Takes them and examines them.*) John Driscoll, you are in my power at last. Nothing can save you now but your sister's promise to become my wife. Here, Teddy (*hands him mask and pistols*), put them back where you found them. (TEDDY *places them in hollow of tree again.*) I'll send the soldiers here to arrest him at once. (*Savagely.*) John Driscoll, your doom is sealed. When you are languishing behind prison bars, we'll see if pretty Aline will refuse me again. (*Shakes his fist at house.*) I hold your brother's life in my hands, proud girl; and if you refuse to wed me I will crush him as I would a worm.

TED. An' what will ye do, squire?

SQU. Marry Aline, by fair means or foul. If she consents, in order to save his life, well and good.

TED. An' if she refuses ye?

SQU. (*savagely*). Crush her brother, and marry her in spite of everything.

TED. An' squire, dear?

SQU. What is it?

TED. Can't we arrest Barney at the same time?

SQU. Not just at present. We have nothing to do with him.

TED. But shure I have a grudge to settle with him.

SQU. For the present let it rest. Now, Teddy. you stay here and watch. I'm going after a warrant and the soldiers.

TED. Don't forget the warrant, squire.

SQU. Never fear, Teddy. Keep a good lookout. And, above all, learn as much as you can. (*Exit, road* R.)

TED. Thrust me, squire. (*Looks around and then goes to pump and fills dipper full of water and holds it in his hand.*) Oh, if I could only get the upper hand of Barney.

(*Enter* KATE *from house,* L.)

KATE. An' what would the likes of ye be afther doin?

TED. (*dropping dipper in a fright*). Nothin'. me pretty girl.

KATE. What are ye doin' there? Spyin' as usual?

TED. Ye hurt me feelin's. me girl, by such base insinuations.

KATE. 'Pon me word, Teddy Burke, ye're gettin' shmart, with yer big words.

TED. (*bowing*). Miss Kate, ye do me proud.

KATE. Oh, do I now?

TED. Ye know I'm not as black as I'm said to be.

KATE. Well, yer not far from it. What were ye sayin' about Barney?

TED. Nothin', Miss Kate. I assure ye.

KATE. I don't believe ye. (*Warningly.*) But look out that he don't hurt ye whin he finds ye.

TED. Have no fear of me, Miss Kate. Barney an' I are the best of friends.

KATE. Oh, ye think so, do ye?

TED. I'm shure of it. An' do ye know, Miss Kate, Barney tould me to make love to ye if I could.

KATE. Oh, he did, did he?

TED. Yis, me darlin'.

KATE (*listening*). I think he's comin' now. We'll ask him.

TED. (*frightened*). I'm in a hurry just now. Some other time will do as well. (*Exit*, R. 3 E., *in a hurry.*)

(*Enter* BARNEY *from house*, L.)

KATE (*looking after* TEDDY). Shure he's afraid to meet Barney.

BAR. Kate Kelley, was that Teddy Burke I just saw ye talkin' to?

KATE. Of course it was.

BAR. O Kate, I niver thought ye'd come to that.

KATE. What do ye mane, Barney?

BAR. (*lighting pipe*). That ye'd so far forget yerself as to talk to the likes of him.

KATE. Oh, indade!

BAR. Yis, Kate, I'm astonished at ye.

KATE. Miss Kate, if ye plaze.

BAR. Would ye listen to that, now. Miss Kate, is it? Me, oh, my, but we're gittin' high up in the world!

KATE. Yis, indade! An' I have been sariously thinkin' of marryin' Teddy Burke.

BAR. Faith an' ye ought. Shure it's a great ladies' man Teddy is entirely.

KATE. Ye may well say so, Barney.

BAR. Misther Donovan, if ye plaze.

KATE (*bowing*). Oh, Misther Donovan, sor.

BAR. That's betther. An' do ye know, Miss Kate, I've sariously been thinkin' of gittin' married meself.

KATE. Oh, have yez. An' who is the girl pray?

BAR. (*aside*). What the divil is her name? (*Aloud.*) Well, folks here about calls her Mona Desmond.

KATE (*in an angry tone*). What are ye sayin', Barney?

BAR. (*coolly*). Fact, I assure ye.

KATE (*crying*). But I was only jokin', Barney.

BAR. Don't cry, acushla! Shure I knew it all the time.

KATE. Do ye mane it?

BAR. Yis; thruly. But, Kate asthore.

KATE. Yis, Barney.

BAR. What was Teddy doin' around here?

KATE. Spyin', I think.

BAR. I fear there's throuble brewin' for the young masther.

KATE. Why do ye think so, Barney?

BAR. (*looking around cautiously*). Lasht night whin the young masther returned from the meetin' I'd a-swore some one was follerin' him. Afther he wint in the house, I came out an' hunted around but found no one. I suppose I was mistaken. But come down the road a piece of the ways, an' maybe we'll find some clew. (*Exeunt down road, L.*)

(*Enter NELLIE from road, R.*)

NEL. (*looking around*). And this is where he lives. (*Enters gate C.*) I wonder how many really know him as he is? Very few, I am afraid. And it was he who at the risk of his life saved mine. (*Shudders.*) Can I ever forget that terrible night on the mountain, when the driver was thrown from his seat, and the frightened horses ran away? How swiftly they went! I closed my eyes, expecting every moment to be dashed into eternity, when suddenly I heard the clatter of an approaching steed. I opened my eyes and looked from the carriage window. What a welcome sight greeted me. There at the heads of the frightened team was a masked man, mounted on a large black steed. Soon the carriage came to a standstill. Placing a whistle to his lips he blew a shrill blast. He then assisted me to alight. I now perceived a second masked man approaching. To him my rescuer gave charge of the carriage and horses. When the first masked man beheld my face, he muttered something under his breath, and removed his hat. This strange being then called me by name, and offered to accompany me home. I gladly accepted his offer, and we started down the mountain. After an hour's walk we reached my father's house. Here he bade me good-night, and lifted his hat. In so doing his mask became loosened and fell from his face. He quickly replaced it, but not before I caught a glimpse of his features. And it is to warn him of danger — the man that saved my life — I come here to-day. If father should find me here, what would he do? I dare not think of the consequences.

(*Enter JOHN from R.*)

JOHN (*entering gate C.*). Good-morning, Miss Shannon. (*Lifts hat.*)

NEL. (*looking around at sound of voice*). Captain Jack!

JOHN (*in a whisper*). Hush! John Driscoll, if you please. No one but you suspects that the hunted rebel and John Driscoll are one and the same person.

NEL. Pardon me, but you startled me so. (*Pityingly.*) Mr. Driscoll, I pity you.

JOHN. Thank you, Miss Shannon, but I'm in need of no sympathy. I am able to take care of myself.

NEL. But there are spies lurking around who would only be too willing to hand you over to the soldiers and receive the reward offered for your capture.

JOHN. Very true. But as I said before, I can take care of myself.

NEL. Mr. Driscoll, I wish to thank you for saving my life. I owe you a debt I can never repay.

JOHN. I but did my duty, Miss Shannon, and I beg of you to mention it no more.

NEL. Mr. Driscoll, you are an honor to the land that gave you birth, and if all Irishmen were as brave as you are, Ireland would be one of the greatest nations on earth.

JOHN. Miss Shannon, is it to thank me and tell me how good I am, you came here this morning?

NEL. No, Mr. Driscoll; something far different.

JOHN (*in surprise*). Indeed!

NEL. (*looking around*). I come to warn you of danger.

JOHN (*in surprise*). Warn me of danger?

NEL. (*in a whisper*). Yes. Your retreat in the mountains has been discovered. To-night when your band is assembled at the meeting, the soldiers will be close at hand to make prisoners of all!

JOHN (*in amazement*). In God's name, who has betrayed us? (*Savagely.*) Which of my men is guilty of such a deed? Tell me his name, and I'll tear him limb from limb.

NEL. Your men are all faithful, Mr. Driscoll.

JOHN. Then it was discovered by accident?

NEL. No, sir; it was no accident. It was found by a spy of the soldiers and police.

JOHN. A spy? Who is it?

NEL. Teddy Burke.

JOHN (*savagely*). Curse him! I should have known it was he. It's such Irishmen as he that have left Ireland the downtrodden nation it is. (*Suddenly.*) But it's strange that you, a girl, should know all this.

NEL. (*laughing*). From your words, Mr. Driscoll, one would suppose our sex had no right to be on earth.

JOHN. Pardon me, Miss Shannon. But still I must confess it's a puzzle to me.

NEL. You forget, sir, my father is head of the soldiers and police.

JOHN. So he is, Miss Shannon.

NEL. This morning I overheard a conversation between my father and Teddy. I heard Teddy tell how he had found the rebels' hiding-place. Then he promised to guide the soldiers there to-night.

JOHN. I'll foil them and their schemes. Forewarned is said to be forearmed, you know.

NEL. In your case I hope so. And now that you are warned, be on your guard.

JOHN. Trust me for that.

NEL. I must be going now, or father will miss me. Good-by. Mr. Driscoll, and good luck be with you. (*Exit by road*, R.)

JOHN (*bowing and lifting hat*). Good-by, Miss Shannon. (*Looks after her.*) Charming girl, a very queen among women. A prize worthy of any man. (*Sighs.*) Ah, well! what right have I to think of her? What am I but a poor, hunted outlaw, with a price on my head. Does she ever think of me as I do of her? No. no. My God, it's impossible! Her father's hatred of the Irish race, I fear, is too deeply planted in the heart of his child. She gave me this warning out of gratitude for saving her life. (*Lightly.*) So far as that goes we are even. (*Stands at gate*, C., *and looks off* R.)

(*Enter* ALINE *and* CAPTAIN *from house*, L.)

CAP. For the present, Miss Aline, I must say adieu, and return to my soldiers.

AL. And you will forgive me for the joke I played on you?

CAP. (*laughing*). Oh, with all my heart.

AL. I am sorry, captain, you must leave us so soon. (*Looks around.*) Why, here's brother John now!

CAP. (*in delight*). John, don't you know me?

JOHN (*coming down*). Edward Gordon!

CAP. (*shaking hands*). The same old Ned as of yore.

JOHN. What are you doing in this part of the world, and in the uniform of an English officer?

CAP. I was sent here to try and find Captain Jack and his men. Knowing at the same time you lived here, I determined to look you up.

JOHN (*slowly*). You have been sent here to hunt down the rebel leader and his men?

CAP. Yes; that is why I'm here.

JOHN (*to* ALINE). You hear that, Aline? He comes here chasing rebels.

CAP. Miss Aline, don't judge me too harshly, I beg of you. I am going to leave the army in a short time. I am sick and tired of hunting men. What are they fighting for but their own?

JOHN. God bless you, Edward, for those words! You have spoken like a man.

AL. (*fervently*). Captain Gordon, you should claim Ireland as your home.

CAP. I sincerely wish I could, Miss Aline. And, to repeat the words of my friend Barney: " Be the great O'Hara! I know some purty colleen I'd be over head an' heels in love with."

AL. (*holding down her head*). O captain!

JOHN. Don't blush, Aline; they well become you. I'm sure you will like Edward when you know him better.

CAP. Don't tease her, John.

JOHN (*laughing*). You hear that, Aline? The captain is taking your part already. I must look sharp, or I'll soon be without a sister.

AL. (*pouting*). O John, how you talk!

CAP. Never mind him, Miss Aline. Brothers are privileged characters, you know. (*Walks to gate,* C.) I must be off now. John, will you accompany me down the road part of the way? We can have a quiet chat over our old college days.

JOHN. With all my heart.

CAP. (*lifting cap*). Good-by, Miss Aline.

AL. Good-by Captain Gordon, and don't forget Kate Kelley and her wedding gift.

CAP. (*laughing*). I'll not forget in a hurry. Come along, John. (*Exit down road,* R.)

AL. Suppose the soldiers should find out brother John was really the rebel leader, Captain Jack, and arrest him? What would become of me? I dread to think of it. I have not a single friend in the world but my brother. And he in the custody of the soldiers, I would indeed be alone and friendless. (*Lightly.*) But pshaw! My fears are groundless. No one suspects him. If they do arrest him, they have no proof of his guilt.

(*Enter* SQUIRE *at gate,* C.)

SQU. (*lifting hat and bowing*). Good-morning, Miss Aline.

AL. (*turns in surprise*). You here, Squire Shannon?

SQU. As you see. You seemed surprised.

AL. (*coldly*). I am surprised to see the wealthy and much-respected Squire Shannon honor our humble home with a visit.

SQU. (*aside*). Fit to be an empress. (*Aloud.*) I had a special object in making this visit, Miss Aline.

AL. (*aside*). I thought as much. (*Aloud.*) Well, sir?

SQU. Has it ever occurred to you, Miss Aline, that you are growing to be a very beautiful woman?

AL. I have been told so.

SQU. (*aside*). Candid, by George! (*Aloud.*) You are also well educated. Why waste your young life in a miserable place like this, when by marrying a rich man you can have your diamonds, your servants, and horses?

AL. (*coldly*). What do you mean, sir?

SQU. (*passionately*). It means, Aline, I love you as I have never loved woman before. Oh, say the word, sweet Aline, that will make me a happy man!

AL. (*slowly*). Mr. Shannon, I must positively decline your kind offer. I can never bestow my hand where my heart is not.

SQU. You love another then?

AL. You have no right to ask me such a question.

Squ. Have a care, girl. It is far better to make a friend of me than an enemy.

Al. You are beside yourself, sir, when you talk like that.

Squ. Girl, I have sworn to make you my wife by fair means or foul.

Al. (*indignantly*). Sir, you are growing insulting. Do you think I would wed a man of your character, after such words as those? Not if you were the last man on earth.

Squ. Then you think I haven't the power to do as I say? You will have to know me a great deal better, my sweet Aline. I could crush your brother in an instant, girl. I hold his very life in my hands. And, what's more, charming Aline, I have proof of his guilt.

Al. And on those terms you would make me your wife?

(*Enter* John *from road*, R.)

Squ. Yes. It's the only way you can save your brother's life.

Al. And what answer do you think my brother would make to such a proposition?

John (*coming down*). No; a thousand times no. Squire Shannon (*points to gate*, C.), there is the way out. Go, before I am tempted to kick you out.

Squ. (*with hand on gate*). So you refuse me, both of you? Well, so be it. John Driscoll, when next we meet you will be in the grasp of the law as a prisoner. (*Exit by road*, R.)

Al. O John, I am so afraid he will do as he says.

John. Cheer up, Aline. No one suspects I am Captain Jack.

(Teddy *now appears behind tree and listens.*)

Ted. (*aside*). Don't be too shure of that, me fine boy.

Al. But the proof he speaks of?

John. He has no proof, Aline. He said that merely to make you consent.

Ted. (*behind tree, aside*). Did he, though.

John (*cheerfully*). Come, come, Aline, don't be down-hearted. (*Looks off* R. 2 E.) What the devil ails Kate and Barney?

(*Enter* Barney *and* Kate, R. 2 E.)

Bar. (*out of breath*). Run Masther John, the soldiers are comin' here.

Al. My God! John, the man has kept his word.

Kate. Fly masther, dear, an' save yerself.

John (*firmly*). No; I will face it like a man. To keep me a prisoner will require proof of my guilt. They have none. (*To* Barney.) Barney, warn the boys not to meet to-night, as our retreat is known to the soldiers.

BAR. Lave it to me, Masther John.

KATE (*looking off* R. 4. E.). Here's the soldiers.

(*Soldiers enter and face audience. Three on each side of gate*, C. SQUIRE SHANNON *enters gate, followed by* CAPTAIN GORDON.)

SQU. (*pointing to* JOHN). Arrest that man! I accuse him of being Captain Jack, the rebel!

CAP. (*in amazement*). My God! Squire Shannon, there is some terrible mistake here. I know this man. We were boys together.

SQU. (*savagely*). There is no mistake. He is Captain Jack, and no one else. (*To soldiers.*) Men, secure your prisoner.

CAP. (*sternly*). Stop! Squire Shannon, I command these men, and not you. And before I make a prisoner of that man (*points to* JOHN) I must have proof of his guilt.

SQU. Oh, very well. (*Calls.*) Teddy.

TED. (*outside*). I'm comin', sor.

(*Enter* TEDDY, *from* R. 3. E.)

TED. Here I am, sor.

SQU. The captain wants proof of the prisoner's guilt. Get it for him.

TED. All right, sor. (*Takes things from tree.*) Here they are, sor.

JOHN. Betrayed!

BAR. Ye spyin' divil! (*Rushes at* TEDDY, *who runs behind the soldiers and is safe.*)

AL. (*wildly*). John, you are lost!

SQU. (*to* CAPTAIN). Are you satisfied?

CAP. For the present, yes. Come, John. (*Places hand on his shoulder.*)

JOHN. I'm ready, captain. (*Falls in between soldiers.*)

CAP. Miss Aline, have no hard feelings against me. I never felt so mean before in all my life. (*Quickly.*) By Jove! I'll leave the army this very day. Cheer up, Miss Aline; your brother is not convicted yet.

BAR. (*warmly*). An' he niver will be.

SQU. (*sternly*). Enough of this. Away with him!

AL. Oh, my heart is breaking. (*Falls fainting in* BARNEY'S *arms.*)

CAP. (*to soldiers*). Forward! March! (*Soldiers march off with prisoner, followed by the* SQUIRE *and* TEDDY. BARNEY *stands* L., *watching them, with* ALINE *in his arms.* KATE *is standing* R., *with apron to her eyes, crying. Slow music at curtain.*)

SLOW CURTAIN.

ACT II.

SCENE. — *A room; doors* L. *and* R. 2. E. *and* R. 4. E; *a writing-desk at* L. 2. E. ; *bookcase* L. C. ; *lounge* R C.: *large window in* C. *to open ; chairs around room ; carpet on floor. Music, " Last Rose of Summer," at rise.*

SQUIRE SHANNON (*at desk writing as curtain rises*).   So far all my plans have succeeded admirably.   John Driscoll is now a pris- oner, accused of being Captain Jack, the outlaw of the mountains. With her brother out of the way, Aline is now left with no one to defend her.   Once the sentence of death is pronounced against him, and John Driscoll is as good as dead, unless she consents to be my wife.   (*Suddenly.*)   And that young officer, Captain Gor- don, is the only man I fear in Ireland, and I know not why.   Will he resign his position in the army as he said he would?   And why does he do so?   Is it that he may be free to make love to Aline? Alas! I fear so.   He knows well she could never love the man who was instrumental in hunting her brother to his doom.   (*Savagely.*) But I'll keep an eye on him and spoil his little game.   And what of Teddy?   I haven't seen him since the time of the arrest this morning.

(*Enter* MARY, *door* L .)

MARY.   Teddy Burke wants to see you, sir.
SQU.   Show him in, Mary.
MARY.   Yes, sir.   (*Exit door* L.)
SQU.   Now I'll hear all the news.   Teddy is a man that never misses anything in the line of hearing.

(*Enter* TEDDY, *door* L.)

TEDDY (*sits down*).   Oh, but I'm tired !.   Shure me legs can hardly hold me up.
SQU.   Where have you been since morning, Teddy ?

(MARY *enters with a lighted lamp, which she places on the desk, and retires.*)

TED.   Takin' care of yer interests, sor.   (*Looks at desk.*)
SQU.   What is it you want, Teddy?
TED.   Somethin' to drink, sor.   I'm parched in the throat.
SQU.   Oh, I see.   (*Calls.*)   Mary !

(*Enter* MARY, *door* L.)

MARY.   Well, sir?
SQU.   Bring us something to drink.
MARY.   Yes, sir.

TED. An' let it be shtrong, me jewel. (*She looks at him indignantly, and exit door*, L., *as he kisses his hand to her*.)

SQU. You admire that girl, Teddy?

TED. I admire all the lovely girls.

(MARY *enters with bottle and glasses, which she places on desk, and exit*, L.)

SQU. Help yourself, Teddy.

TED. Thank you, sor. (*Fills glass and holds it up*.) Here's to yer honor's health. (*Drinks*.) Ah, that makes a new man of me. (*Places glass down*.)

SQU. Now, what have you to say?

TED. This mornin', afther John Driscoll was arrested an' placed in the prison, I undertook to see what Captain Gordon was goin' to do. Afther follerin' him for a while he gave me the shlip.

SQU. The captain is a sharp one.

TED. Ye may well say so, yer honor.

SQU. What did you do when you found you had lost track of him?

TED. Thin I turned me attention to Barney. But the divil a sight of him could I find.

SQU. (*in surprise*). What became of him?

TED. Divil a one of me knows. But I suppose he wint up the mountains an' warned the rebels not to meet to-night.

SQU. (*slowly*). Do you really think so?

TED. I'm positive of it, sor.

SQU. Then it will be useless to send the soldiers after them.

TED. I agree with ye, sor. The soldiers might run into a thrap, squire.

SQU. Very true, Teddy. And furthermore, Barney must have warned them by this.

TED. Of course he has, an' long ago. For ye know Barney is hand an' glove with his masther.

SQU. (*savagely*). Curse him. If I could only find some proof of Barney's guilt, I'd have him in a cell in no time.

TED. Ye'll niver do it, squire. He is too cute, an' covers up his thracks too well.

SQU. I'll get the best of him yet, or my name is not Jim Shannon.

TED. I hope so, squire. (*Shaking head*.) But I doubt if ye iver will.

SQU. What did you do when you found Barney had given you the slip also?

TED. I returned to the prison, an' was just in time to hear the sentence of death pronounced against John Driscoll, for being a rebel.

SQU. (*jumping up*). What! Has he been tried already?

TED. Yis, yer honor.

SQU. My God! But this is sudden.

TED. (*rubbing his hands*). Ye forget, squire, the law in Ireland makes short work of a rebel.

SQU. (*walking up and down*). When is he to die?

TED. He will be shot at sunrise in the mornin'.

SQU. Well, so be it. (*Sits down.*) The sooner he dies the better for all hands concerned in the plot. Teddy, you keep a close watch on the prison to-night. Have the soldiers in readiness to frustrate all attempts at a rescue. I am afraid of Barney and his friends.

TED. Why so, squire?

SQU. They might undertake to liberate the prisoner during the night.

TED. Oh, yis; to be shure.

SQU. Be off with you, now. And, above all, see that the rebel don't escape.

TED. (*rising*). I'll see iverythin' is all right in the mornin'. (*Exit door, L.*)

SQU. (*solus*). So John Driscoll will be shot to-morrow, will he? Well, perhaps 'tis better so. And what of Aline? Will she become my wife to save her brother, when she finds he has been condemned as a rebel and must die? I wonder if she'll come to me and beg of me to save him? (*Strikes desk with fist.*) By George! if she don't come to-night I'll have to get the judge to reprieve the prisoner for a few days.

(*Enter* NELLIE, *door* R. 2 E.)

NELLIE (*seeing her father*). You here, father? (*Sits down.*)

SQU. Yes, my child. (*Looks at her.*) You are pale. Are you ill? Speak, Nellie, I implore you.

NEL. No, father; I am as well as ever.

SQU. Then what seems to be the matter?

NEL. (*in a weary tone*). I don't know, father. Perhaps it's the news I've just heard.

SQU. (*in surprise*). News! What news?

NEL. (*in astonishment*). Haven't you heard that John Driscoll has been condemned?

SQU. Indeed! (*Sternly.*) And why should you feel any pity for him? Remember, he is a rebel.

NEL. I know he is accused of being one. But I do pity him, father, from the bottom of my heart. And if he is the man they accuse him of being, what was he fighting for but his own? A man condemned without a trial. I don't blame the Irish rebels for fighting as long as they have a drop of blood in their veins.

SQU. (*in amazement*). Well, 'pon my word, if you're not the worst little rebel of them all.

NEL. (*shaking her head*). I am no rebel, father. But my sympathies are with the oppressed and down-trodden.

SQU. Have a care, girl. You know such words are treasonable.

NEL. I care not.

SQU. (*rising*). I am going to my room for a while, Nellie. You remain here, and if any one calls to see me let me know. (*Exit door*, R. 2 E.)

NEL. (*clasping her hands*). O God! To think that John Driscoll must die like a dog! Is there no way in which he can escape? (*Sadly.*) Alas! I fear not. But why should I give up? While there is life there is hope. (*Quickly.*) I know what I will do. I'll send for Barney. He must know of some way in which Mr. Driscoll can receive assistance from the outside. (*Calls.*) Mary!

(*Enter* MARY, *door* L.)

MARY. Well, miss.

NEL. Mary, I want you to do me a favor.

MARY. Yes, miss; if I can.

NEL. Where is Tim?

MARY. In the stable-yard, miss.

NEL. Mary, I want you to send Tim to me. And, above all, don't let my father see the person Tim will bring home with him. And, Mary, this is for your trouble. (*Takes off ring and places it on* MARY'S *finger.*)

MARY. Oh, thank you, miss. (*Exit* MARY, *door* L.)

NEL. I'll send Tim to find Barney and bring him here. And between the two of us arrange a plan for the escape of Mr. Driscoll.

(*Enter* TIM, *door* L.)

TIM BURNS. Here I am, miss.

NEL. Tim, you know where to find Barney Donovan?

TIM. Faith an' I do, miss.

NEL. Now, Tim, I want you to hunt Barney up and bring him here as soon as possible.

TIM. I understand ye, miss. But how about yer fayther seein' him? Ye know he has no love for Barney.

NEL. True for you, Tim. But have no fear; I'll arrange all that. Barney need not enter the house so that father can see him. (*Points to window*, C.) Look! Yonder window opens on the lawn. He can enter there. I will be here to receive him.

TIM. Of course, miss.

NEL. And, Tim, tell him to hurry, please, as it may be the means of saving the life of one he loves.

TIM. I'm off like a shot, miss.

NEL. Go! (*Fervently.*) And may heaven guide thy steps.

TIM. Amen to that, miss. Shure, I'll be back in no time. (*Exit, door* L.)

NEL. If Tim should fail? No, no; the thought is maddening. John Driscoll must escape to-night. Ay, even if I have to take his place in the morning.

(Enter MARY, *door* L.)*

MARY. Captain Gordon wishes to see your father, miss.

NEL. Show the gentleman in, Mary.

MARY. Yes, miss. *(Exit, door* L.)

NEL. Does Captain Gordon come to intercede for the prisoner? I sincerely hope so.

(Enter CAPTAIN, *door* L.)*

CAP. *(bowing and lifting hat).* Good-evening, Miss Shannon. I beg your pardon for intruding; but I was given to understand, by the servant, that your father awaited me here.

NEL. *(rising).* Father is in his room. Be seated, please, and I will send him to you in a moment. *(Exit, door* R. 2 E.)

CAP. *(sits down).* Deuced pretty girl, and fit to make any man happy for life. And yet she is not half as charming as my Aline asthore.

(Enter SQUIRE, *door* R. 2 E.)*

SQU. Ah, captain, glad to see you. *(Sits down.)* Where is your uniform, Captain Gordon? *(Looking at him in astonishment.)*

CAP. Don't call me captain, and don't speak to me of a uniform. I am no longer a soldier of the English government.

SQU. Captain, you astonish me.

CAP. There is no need of being astonished, squire. Everything is just as I have said.

SQU. Why have you left the army, Mr. Gordon?

CAP. Because I am sick and tired of being an instrument of the government in hunting to death the rebels of Ireland.

SQU. *(aside).* Words of treason. *(Aloud.)* You forget, Mr. Gordon, they are conspiring against the crown.

.CAP. Conspiring fiddlesticks! They are fighting for their own. Why don't England allow Ireland home rule as well as Scotland?

SQU. Because Ireland, as a nation, has no men of brains.

CAP. Squire Shannon, you utter a falsehood when you say so. Ireland has sons and daughters as brilliant as any England ever boasted of. And it's for this reason — and this alone — that Ireland has for ages been ground in the dust by the heel of oppression.

SQU. Oh, indeed!

CAP. Yes, indeed! You know every word I speak is the gospel truth. But I came to speak of something different from Ireland's wrongs.

SQU. *(in surprise).* Yes. What is it you wish?

CAP. That John Driscoll be reprieved.

SQU. Why should I interest myself in him. The rebel had a fair trial.

CAP. Yes; a mock trial, you mean. The judge knew the sentence of death was to be pronounced on John before the trial took place at all.

SQU.   He had a fair and impartial trial, and must now suffer the consequences of being an outlaw.

CAP.   Squire Shannon, how do you know he is an outlaw? What proof have you to show of his guilt ?

SQU.   The mask and revolvers found in the hollow of the tree.

CAP.   They might have been placed there by an enemy of his.

SQU.   How about the conversation overheard by Teddy?

CAP.   To what conversation do you refer?

SQU.   Where John Driscoll admitted to his sister Aline that he was the rebel leader, Captain Jack.

CAP.   And what is Teddy but a spy and informer?

SQU.   You forget he was under oath when he gave his evidence.

CAP.   And is it on the evidence of such a man as Teddy Burke they are going to shoot him?   I wouldn't believe a word Teddy spoke, if he swore to it on a stack of Bibles as high as himself.

SQU.   I am sorry, Mr. Gordon ; but the rebel must die in the morning.

CAP.   But his sentence might be delayed for a few days at least.

SQU. (*shaking his head*).   I am afraid not.   I hardly think the judge would grant him a reprieve.

CAP.   But influence might be brought to bear on the case.

SQU.   Very true.   But where will the man of influence be found, I'd like to know?

CAP.   Squire Shannon, you are high in the affairs of the government.

SQU.   In some things, yes.   In others, no.

CAP.   You can intercede for him with the judge.   And I am positive you will do his sister Aline a great favor at the same time.

SQU. (*shaking his head*).   I can do nothing.   •

CAP. (*rising*).   Then you refuse ?

SQU.   I must in this case.   The prisoner has been tried and condemned as a rebel, fighting against the English government.   If he was to go free, of what use would judges and juries be in Ireland?

CAP.   To convict innocent men and earn blood-money.   (*Sternly.*) But I tell you this much, Jim Shannon, the prisoner will not die at sunrise.   Mark well what I say, for I make no idle boast.

SQU. (*rising*).   What do you mean, sir?

CAP.   You have heard what I said.   Good-night.   (*Exit, door* L.)

SQU. (*sits down*).   I don't like that man at all.   He is the only man I ever met I am afraid of, and I know not why.   Curse him ! I wish I could have him shot in the morning also.   What did he mean by saying the prisoner would not die to-morrow?   Is there any fear that Driscoll may escape in the night?

(*Enter* MARY, *door* L.)

MARY.   A young woman wishes to see you, sir.

SQU.   What is her name?

MARY. She gave no name, sir.

SQU. (*aside*). It must be Aline at last. (*Aloud.*) Show the young woman in, Mary.

MARY. Yes, sir. (*Exit, door* L.)

SQU. (*in joyful tones*). At last she is here to beg for her brother's life. I wonder if she will consent to be my wife? If she does, he shall receive a pardon. If not, then he dies.

(*Enter* ALINE, *door* L.)

ALINE (*falling on her knees*). O Mr. Shannon, please save my brother!

SQU. Rise, Miss Aline, and be seated. Do not kneel to any one but God, who sees us all. (*Aside.*) That speech will make her regard me in a different light.

AL. (*sits down*). Then you will save him, sir? (*Appealingly.*) Oh, say you will!

SQU. Impossible! The sentence of death has been pronounced against him, and he must die.

AL. Is there no hope?

SQU. I fear not. (*Then quickly.*) But stay! There is a way.

AL (*quickly*). Yes, yes; tell it to me quickly.

SQU. Miss Aline, now I come to think of it, I can and will save him on one condition.

AL. Name the condition, Squire Shannon, and if it's in my power, it shall be done at once.

SQU. No rash promise, Miss Aline.

AL. I will do as I say, sir.

SQU. Very good. You remember the proposition I made to you this morning at your home?

AL. (*bowing*). I do.

SQU. It still holds good. Promise to become my wife, and your brother is a free man. (*Savagely.*) Refuse, and he dies the death of a dog.

AL. My God! man, are you human?

SQU. I am. But my love for you makes a perfect demon of me. (*Appealingly.*) Say you will become my wife, Aline, and save your brother's life. Remember, on your answer depends his fate.

AL. No, no. I cannot consent to such a thing.

SQU. Not even for his sake?

AL. No; not even for his sake. You ask too much. (*Rising.*) I will now quit the presence of the man I loathe and fear. Squire Shannon, you are nothing but a contemptible cur!

SQU. (*rising and locking door*, L.). Not so fast my pretty maid. You are in my power at last, Aline.

AL. Squire Shannon, you lie!

SQU. (*laughing*). Oh, do I? We shall see if I do.

AL. (*in alarm*). What do you mean. sir?

SQU. I mean you will never leave this house until you promise to become my wife.

AL. (*looking around*). Would you dare make a prisoner of me?

SQU. Aline, I would do anything for the woman I love. Ay, even to keeping her a prisoner for years, or until one or the other of us shall die.

AL. I will scream for help.

SQU. No use of wasting your breath in screaming, Aline. No one will hear you. There is a nice little cage up-stairs that will hold you tightly. Come with me, sweet Aline, and I will show it to you. (*Takes her by the arm.*)

AL. (*shrinking back*). Don't you dare lay a hand on me.

SQU. (*takes hold of her again*). Aline, you had better come willingly, or I will be forced to carry you.

AL. (*breaks away*). Never, sir.

SQU. (*angrily*). I've stood this long enough. Come with me you must. (*Takes hold of her and both struggle.*)

AL. (*struggling*). O God! Will no one help me? (*Cries out.*) Help! help! (*Appealingly.*) O God, will no one save me? (*Struggles all the time.*)

SQU. No; not one. You are here alone and friendless.

(*Enter* CAPTAIN *at window*, C.)

CAP. (*dashes window open and jumps into room*). You lie, you-devil! (SQUIRE *releases* ALINE; *she runs to* CAPTAIN, *who puts his arm around her waist.*)

SQU. Curse you, Gordon! Are you here again? What do you want? (*Savagely.*) Release that girl, before I ring and have the servants throw you off my grounds. (*Places hand on bell-rope hanging on the wall.*)

CAP. (*points revolver at him*). Don't touch it, squire. I hate to send a man of your stamp to an early grave, but if you don't remove your hand in double quick time, there will be a funeral in your family, and you will be the centre of attraction. (SQUIRE *removes his hand.*) Look out, Shannon, how you behave; I'm going to keep an eye on you in the future. (*Moves to window*, C.) Come, Aline; this is no place for you. Your honor, we both bid you a very good-night. (*Exeunt through window*, C.)

SQU. (*jumping up*). Curse him! I'll have her back before he can leave the grounds. (*Savagely.*) And I will have his life in the bargain. If he should be killed in leaving, I'll say the servants mistook him for a poacher in the dark, and shot him by mistake. (*Exit, door* L., *after unlocking it.*)

(*Enter* BARNEY, *window* C.)

BAR. (*looking around cautiously*). An' ye'll have the young captain shot for a poacher, will ye? I wonder what would the squire say if he knew I was under the winder for the last half-hour. (*Laughing.*) Shure, he might have me shot for a poacher, too. Arrah, but didn't the youngster cool him down in good style. An' the squire is goin' to send the servants afther the captain an' Miss Aline, is he? Shure, there ain't a servant in the house but Mary. This is a fine house entirely. (*Looks around.*) I wonder what's in the bottle? (*Goes to desk and smells of it.*) Whiskey! Well, here's to the squire's health. (*Drinks.*) Ah, that's the stuff for me. (*Listens.*) Footsteps, be the harp of Tara! (*Jumping around.*) I must get out of this in a hurry. (*Looking around.*) Where can I hide? I will go in here. (*Exit, door* R. 4 E.)

(*Enter* NELLIE, *door* R. 2 E.)

NEL. (*sits down*). Oh, dear, what keeps Barney from coming? Was it possible that Tim couldn't find him? I sincerely hope not. O Barney, Barney, where are you?

BAR. (*re-entering*). Here, acushla!

NEL. (*in amazement*). How long have you been in that room? And how did you get in.

BAR. Hold on, avick. One question at a time. I came in through yonder winder. An', be the token, I also hope to lave the same way. I was in the room whin I heard ye approachin', an' as I thought it might be yer fayther I lift as fast as I could.

NEL. (*laughing*). Then you are afraid of my father?

BAR. Well, not that I know of. But shtill I'd rather be at a distance whin he's around.

NEL. Barney, I'm glad you are here. I want to see if we can't do something for your master.

BAR. (*in surprise*). Me masther?

NEL. Why, yes; Mr. Driscoll.

BAR. (*in astonishment*). Miss Shannon, ye don't mane ye'd help him to escape?

NEL. Why not? You know he saved my life at the risk of his own, and I am going to do all in my power to save him.

BAR. But what will yer fayther say whin he finds it out? Remember, he is a stern man, an' never forgives any one who crosses his path.

NEL. He need know nothing of it whatever. Now, Barney, think of some way in which he can escape.

BAR. There is one way it might be done.

NEL. Yes, yes.

BAR. To shtay an' be shot. Shure, thin he could escape from this world to the next.

NEL. O Barney, do be serious for once in your life! This is no time for joking.

BAR. For yer sake, acushla, I will.

NEL. Thank you, Barney. Now think of some scheme that might benefit Mr. Driscoll.

BAR. (*slowly*). Miss Shannon, I am sorry to say he is beyond all help!

NEL. (*sadly*). O Barney, don't say he is dead!

BAR. (*laughing*). Arrah, no! Masther John escaped over an hour ago.

NEL. (*fervently*). Thank God!

BAR. (*aside*). She loves him, then. (*Aloud.*) They'll niver shoot Captain Jack at sunrise.

NEL. How did he manage to pass the guards?

BAR. Well, to tell ye the truth, it was an easy thing. I was on bad terms with one of the guards. He saw me prowlin' around the prison, an' ordered me away.

NEL. And did you go, Barney?

BAR. Of course I did — not. I got him away from the rest of them, an' thin downed him. I shtripped him of his uniform, an' thin bound an' gagged him.

NEL. Yes, Barney.

BAR. Ye niver saw me in a uniform, did ye?

NEL. I can't say that I have, but I am sure I would like to.

BAR. Oh, faith, an' I know ye would. I'm a purty sight entirely. Ye'd die of admiration.

NEL. (*laughing*). I suppose so.

BAR. Ye'd be captivated with me. But to continue me shtory. Afther I took his uniform I put it on, an' thin shouldered his musket.

NEL. Weren't you afraid, Barney?

BAR. Divil a bit, accushla.

NEL. I know I should die of fright.

BAR. Even if it was to save the man ye love?

NEL. (*holding down her head*). O Barney.

BAR. Don't mind me, Nellie asthore. Captain Jack is worthy of any girl in Ireland.

NEL. You are right, Barney; Mr. Driscoll is a man among men.

BAR. Faith, an' he is; among the women too.

NEL. Go on, Barney. I won't interrupt you again.

BAR. I took the guard's place in front of the prison, an' began marchin' up an' down in front of the door.

NEL. What door, Barney?

BAR. The cell door, of course. Every time I passed I would give a little rap on the door with the end of the musket. Afther a while he came to the gratin' an' looked out. I made a sign to him which he recognized at once. I unlocked the door an' let him out. I made him put on the uniform an' take the musket. not forgettin' at the same time the countersign, which I heard the others callin' out, in case he should be challenged by any of the guards. He easily made his escape in the dark, once he was outside the walls.

NEL. And he got away without being detected?

BAR. He did that, an' is at this moment safe an' sound.

NEL. Yes: but, Barney, you were still inside the prison walls. How did you escape?

BAR. I climbed to the top of the wall an' dropped over. In the darkness no one noticed me,

NEL. But the guard? You say you knew him. Might he not tell who liberated the prisoner?

BAR. Oh, he won't say a word.

NEL. But he may out of revenge.

BAR. Not him! Shure, he'd be court-martialled an' shot for lavin' his posht while on juty!

NEL. Where is Mr. Driscoll now?

BAR. Where all the soldiers in Ireland could niver find him. I must be off now, an' see if all is right around the Driscoll homestead.

NEL. Go by all means, Barney. And, Barney, dear —

BAR. Ma'am to ye.

NEL. You will take good care of Mr. Driscoll? For soon the hue and cry will be raised when his escape has been made known.

BAR. (*aside*). The little witch! (*Aloud.*) I'll see that no harm comes to him, for yer sake, acushla.

NEL. Do; and may heaven bless you, Barney Donovan.

BAR. Good-night, asthore. (*Exit, window* C.)

NEL. Good-night. (*Solus.*) When morning dawns won't there be a surprise in store for John Driscoll's enemies, when his escape is made known. (*Rising.*) I'm so happy. I don't know what to do. (*Exit, door* R. 2 E.)

(*Enter* SQUIRE, *door* L.)

SQU. Not a blamed servant in the house but Mary. After hunting all over I found her, only to learn the others had gone to a wake. Why the deuce can't people live, and save other people the time wasted in going to their wake? Nice fix to be in, I must say. (*Sits down.*) I suppose by this time Captain Gordon and Aline are a good ways from here. It's no use. the sentence of Captain Jack must be delayed for a few days at least. Aline must and shall become my wife. I had her in my power to-night, and would have made her consent but for that meddling Captain Gordon. (*Savagely.*) Curse him! I wish the Devil had him in, his grip. And how blind I have been not to have discovered it before, that my daughter Nellie was in love with John Driscoll! Where and when they became acquainted is what beats me. This must be looked into. Well, well, what a strange world we live in! Well, Mary?

(*Enter* MARY, *door* L.)

MARY. Teddy has come, sir.

SQU. Let him come in.

MARY. Yes, sir. (*Exit, door* L.)

SQU. I wonder what brings him here now.

(*Enter* TEDDY, *door* L.)

TED. O squire, have ye heard the news?

SQU. What news?

TED. John Driscoll has escaped!

SQU. (*jumping up*). What!

TED. Yis, squire; it's thrue.

SQU. (*walking up and down*). How long has he been gone?

TED. The guard has just been found, bound hand an' foot. He says some one knocked him senseless more than an hour ago. Who it was that struck him he don't know.

SQU. Have the soldiers been ordered out after the prisoner?

TED. They have, sor.

SQU. Good! We'll have him back yet.

TED. I hope so, squire. I won't be safe in Ireland, with him at liberty, afther the evidence I gave.

SQU. Have no fear, Teddy, I'll see you are taken care of.

TED. Thank ye, squire.

SQU. I must not let Nellie know of his escape. She is getting to be such an infernal little rebel.

TED. She takes great interest in Captain Jack.

SQU. She merely pities him, that is all.

TED. Maybe it's more than pity, squire.

SQU. What do you mean, Teddy Burke?

TED. There is such a word as love, sor.

SQU. Why, Teddy, you must be dreaming. My daughter is a stranger as yet to John Driscoll.

TED. Remember, sur, there is such a thing as love at first sight.

SQU. Yes, but not in this case. Why, I would rather see my child dead at my feet, than married to an Irish rebel!

TED. That may be all very well, sor. But girls of nowadays are different from what they used to be. It's the heart they consult now, an' not the parents, in the choosin' of a husband. An' I don't think it would be out of the way in keepin' an eye on her.

SQU. (*impatiently*). Don't be a fool, Teddy!

TED. Have it yer own way, sor.

SQU. Drop the subject altogether. Let us go and see how the man-hunt is progressing.

TED. With all me heart. For on the capture of Driscoll, depends me safety.

SQU. Then come on. (*Exit, door* L.)

(*Enter* NELLIE, *door* R. 2 E.)

NEL. Won't father be mad when he hears of the escape of Captain Jack. I wonder where Mr. Driscoll is now?

(*Enter* JOHN DRISCOLL, *window*, C.)

JOHN. Here, Miss Shannon!

NEL. (*startled*). John — I mean Mr. Driscoll, you here?

JOHN. You may call me John.

NEL. Don't you know you run a terrible danger in coming here? Why do you come?

JOHN. To thank you.

NEL. (*in surprise*). Why thank me? What have I done to receive thanks for?

JOHN. Miss Shannon, I met Barney since he came here, and he has told me all.

NEL. (*holding down her head*). Barney has told you all, you say?

JOHN. Yes; everything. And I thank you from the bottom of my heart.

NEL. I was but paying back the debt I owed to you.

JOHN. Miss Shannon, before I leave I wish to say a few words to you. It's true we have been known to each other but a short while; yet in that time I have grown to love you very much. Pardon me for speaking as I do. I know it is impossible for you to love a hunted outlaw like me. All I ask of you is to think of me as you have known me, not as I am painted.

NEL. (*shyly*). But suppose I do love the hunted outlaw, what then?

JOHN (*sighing*). Ah, no; you but jest.

NEL. No, Mr. Driscoll, I am in earnest. (*Passionately.*) John, I have loved you since the night you saved my life.

JOHN. Nellie, do you really mean it?

NEL. I do.

JOHN (*kissing her*). Then there is happiness yet in store for the Irish rebel.

NEL. (*listens; then in alarm*). My father is coming.

JOHN. At that rate I'd better be going. (*Moves to window*, C., *and looks out.*) My God! Nellie, I have been betrayed. What shall I do? The yard is full of soldiers! Where can I hide? I will die before they capture me again.

NEL. (*looking around room*). Hide in here, quick! (*Rushes him into room, door* R. 4 E., *and closes it; then sits at desk and takes up book and pretends to read.*)

(*Enter* SQUIRE, *door* L.)

SQU. Nellie, my child, are you still up? How long have you been here?

NEL. Over an hour, father.

SQU. (*listening*). What is all that loud talking in the yard for? Who's doing it? (*Sits down.*)

NEL. (*rising and laying book on desk*). I'll go and see, sir. (*Goes to window*, C., *and looks out.*) Mercy! The yard is full of soldiers.

SQU. (*jumping up*). Soldiers? What the devil are they doing on my grounds at this time of night?

NEL. (*walking away from window*). Here comes the lieutenant.

(*Enter* LIEUTENANT, *window* C.)

LIEUTENANT ROGERS (*bowing to* NELLIE). Beg pardon, squire, for disturbing you at this late hour; but the fact is, we have tracked Captain Jack to your grounds, and have lost sight of him.

Squ. (*in amazement*). Captain Jack here?

Lieu. He is hiding on your grounds somewhere. Whether he entered the house I can't say. Has this room been occupied all the evening?

Squ. It has.

Lieu. By yourself?

Squ. By myself and daughter. My child has been here while I was not. (*Sternly.*) Nellie, have you seen the outlaw, Captain Jack, to-night?

Lieu. Oh, it's unnecessary for her to answer that question. I'll take it for granted she hasn't seen him.

Squ. But I command her to answer. Girl, have you seen the rebel?

Nel. (*slowly and distinctly*). No, father, I have not seen Captain Jack to-night! (NELLIE *stands* R., *with bowed head; the* SQUIRE, C., *looking at her, and the* LIEUTENANT *at window*, C., *looking at both of them.*)

SLOW CURTAIN.

ACT III.

SCENE. — *Same as Act First. Music, " The Harp of Tara."*

KATE (*at gate* C.). I wonder what became of that divil, Mr. Barney Donovan? I haven't seen him since yesterday mornin'. Shure, there's terrible things goin' on since the young masther was arrested as the rebel leader. (*Sighing.*) Oh, dear, I wonder how it will all end? (*Looks off* R.) Here comes Barney now. I'm so glad to see him again! (*Suddenly.*) I know what I'll do. I'll pretend I'm mad, an' won't I just give it to him.

(*Enter* BARNEY *from* R.)

BAR. Top o' the mornin' to ye, Kate.

KATE. Don't ye dare talk to me, Barney Donovan.

BAR. (*aside*). What the divil ails her now? (*Aloud.*) Kate, acushla, has anythin' disturbed yer peace o' mind?

KATE (*crying*). How dare ye ask me such a question as that? O Barney Donovan, I just hate the sight of ye! Ye can go back as fast as ye came to yer red-headed, squint-eyed Judy Callahan!

BAR. Oh, be the livin' tinker, is it jealous ye are, Kate? Well, well! 'Pon me soul that's the greatest news I've heard in tin years. Oh, did any one ever hear the likes of it? Kate Kelley jealous!

KATE. An' who wouldn't be? Ye are always tellin' me how much ye love me, an' as soon as my back is turned ye are makin' love to some one else. (*Crying.*) O Barney, Barney, ye are breakin' me heart!

BAR. An' I do love ye, avourneen. An' I love ye as dearly an' as thruely as ever man loved woman before. Listen, an' I'll tell ye how much I think of you. (*Sings.*)

> O Katie, acushla, now don't be provokin',
> My heart it's inflamed with the passion of love;
>   Only say yis, an' I'll still keep on hopin',
> Sure my love is as pure as the angels above.
>   Now, Katie, acushla, don't be unrelentin',
> Wherever I go I am thinkin' of you,
>   Sleepin' or wakin' my thoughts you're frequentin',
> O Katie, acushla, are you still true?
>
>   O Katie, acushla, my heart it is breakin',
> Your silence is stronger than words can e'er be;
>   Why don't you list to the promise I'm makin',
> To love you, avourneen, an' none other than thee.
>   Now, Katie, acushla, lave off with yer teasin',
> We'll go to the priest an' it's married we'll be;
>   For, Katie, I know that my presence is pleasin',
> An' we'll leave dear old Erin for the land of the free.

(*Any song may be substituted.*)

KATE (*at end of song; aside*). I feel just like throwin' me arms around his neck an' kissin' him. (*Aloud.*) Oh, it's all very well to tell me how much ye love me; but that don't tell me where ye have been for the past day an' night.

BAR. Oh, that's the cause of the row, is it?

KATE. Ain't that cause enough? I haven't seen ye since the time of the masther's arrist. Now, sor, explain where ye spint the time between thin an' now.

BAR. Watchin' over Masther John. Shure, ye know I am the only frind the masther has.

KATE (*shaking her head*). Thrue for ye, Barney.

BAR. (*looking around*). An' if it hadn't been for me the masther would have been in his grave by this.

KATE (*in surprise*). What do ye mane, Barney Donovan?

BAR. (*in disgust*). Arrah, it must be blind ye are intirely, Kate. Can't ye see beyond yer nose? Shure, it was me that helped the masther escape.

KATE. O Barney! An' ye risked yer life to save his?

BAR. Of course I did. An' what's more I'd do it again.

KATE (*throwing her arms around his neck*). O Barney, I'm so proud of ye. (*Releasing him.*) But is the masther safe?

BAR. What foolish questions ye ask, Kate. Why, shure, the entire English army couldn't find him. But, whist, Kate, I've great news for ye.

KATE (*in surprise*). Ye have?

BAR. Oh, faith, an' I have.

KATE. What kind of news is it? Good or bad, or what?

BAR. It's the best kind of news as far as I'm concerned. Shure, it's no more nor less than Masther John is in love with the squire's daughter.

KATE (*in astonishment*). No?

BAR. Yis; I heard him whin he tould her so.

KATE. An' does she return his love, Barney?

BAR. Well, to tell ye the truth, I don't know what answer she made him in words. But what I did hear was a sound reminding me of a cork bein' pulled from a bottle. Of course ye know what that means.

KATE (*laughing*). O Barney, won't the squire raise a row whin he hears of it?

BAR. I suppose he will. But what can he do? Love laughs at all obstacles, ye know.

KATE. Yis, so I'm tould.

BAR. But, Kate dear, do ye know I'm divilish hungry. I was out all night, an' not a morsel of food has passed me lips in thirty-two hours.

KATE. Serves ye right. Why don't ye eat at regular hours like a dacent person should. (*Pulls him by the arm.*) Come along, though, an I'll try an' fix ye up. (*Exit, into house,* L.)

BAR. (*holding back*). All right, me girl, as soon as I have a drink of water. (*Goes to pump and fills dipper and drinks.*)

(*Enter* CAPTAIN, *at gate,* C.)

CAP. (*looking around and sees* BARNEY). Good-morning, Barney.

BAR. (*turning around*). Ah, captain dear, good-mornin' to ye.

CAP. Is Miss Aline up yet? I wish you'd see. I have a few words to say to her of an important nature.

BAR. Thin ye want to see her, do ye? An' ye want me to tell her yer here, do ye?

CAP. (*bowing*). Yes; if you please.

BAR. All right, sor. I'll have her out here in a second. (*Exit, into house,* L.)

CAP. (*solus*). I am going to declare my love to her. I wonder what she will say? (*Lightly.*) Oh, well, her answer can only be yes or no. (*Seriously.*) And I sincerely hope it will be yes.

(*Enter* ALINE *from house,* L.)

AL. (*seeing* CAPTAIN). Ah, Captain Gordon, you here?

CAP. (*bowing*). Yes. Miss Aline, I came to say good-by. I am going to return to England. I am free to go and come when I like. There is but one thing that can keep me in Ireland longer than to-day. What it is I need not say. I have made up my mind to go, and go I shall.

AL. And why should you leave Ireland, captain?

CAP. Because there is no attachment on account of which I should remain.

AL. But you spoke of some object that might keep you here?

CAP. Yes, Aline — if I might be allowed to call you by that name — there is one.

AL. Yes. And what is that one, if I might be so bold as to ask?

CAP. It means, Aline, I love you dearly, and want you to become my wife. I am not an Irishman by birth, I know; but I am Irish to the backbone at heart. I have only known you a short time, still, in that period, I have grown to love you dearly. Aline, will you marry me?

AL. (*slyly*). Now?

CAP. Well, not just at present.

AL. When?

CAP. That part of the arrangement I'll leave to you. Only let your answer be yes, and make me the happiest of men.

AL. Well, Captain Gordon, I do consent. I have loved you since the time you kissed me for Kate Kelley.

CAP. Then I'll make no mistake this time. (*Clasps her in his arms and kisses her.*) And you will become Mrs. Edward Gordon?

AL. (*laughing*). Why, of course I will.

CAP. (*releases her*). Then, Aline, I think I'll remain in Ireland for the present.

AL. You forget, Edward, my brother John is a fugitive from justice. There is a price on his head. If he is found he will be shot like a dog. To save his life he must leave the land of his birth to become a wanderer in France or America. And where my brother goes I go also.

CAP. Spoken like a true-hearted daughter of Erin's Isle. But, Aline dear.

AL. Yes, Edward.

CAP. I kind of think we'll all remain here for some time yet. I say, I kind of think we will; mind, I don't say for certain.

AL. (*in astonishment*). Why, Edward, what do you mean?

CAP. Nothing just now. I may be all wrong. But I hope not.

AL. Why, how strange you talk. Be more outspoken in your language. Don't clothe your words in mystery.

CAP. Well, the long and the short of it is, Aline, I am going to Dublin to-day.

AL. (*in amazement*). To Dublin!

CAP. Why, yes. You seem surprised.

AL. I must confess I am. Why do you go there?

CAP. To try and get a pardon for your brother John. I have some influence there, and I think I can get a pardon for him and his followers.

AL. Then go at once, and may heaven guide thy feet. Good-by, Edward.

CAP. Good-by, Aline. (*He kisses her, and exit by road,* L.)

AL. O God! I do so hope he will be successful, and can procure a pardon for my brother and his men. If he don't succeed in the undertaking, all we can do is to leave the place of our birth and find a new home in France or America. (*Exit into house,* L.)

(*Enter* SQUIRE *from road*, R.)

SQU. (*at gate*, C.). No one about. Strange where they all can be. I wonder is Teddy on the watch? (*Whistles.*) Ah! he's on guard.

(*Enter* TEDDY *from* R. 3 E.)

TED. Good-mornin', to ye, squire.

SQU. (*angrily*). Bosh! Come to the point at once. Have you been on the watch all night, as I directed?

TED. I have, yer honor.

SQU. You are sure you haven't been asleep?

TED. Divil a wink, sor. I niver slape on me post of duty.

SQU. Any signs of the escaped rebel, Captain Jack?

TED. Not a sign as yet, sor.

SQU. You are sure he didn't slip into the house unknown to you? Remember, the night was very dark.

TED. Squire Shannon, the ribel didn't come near the house durin' the night.

SQU. You are sure?

TED. I am positive, sor.

SQU. Has my daughter Nellie been around here yet?

TED. I haven't seen her this mornin', sor. But, shure, ye don't suspect yer own flesh an' blood, sor?

SQU. Oh, don't I though? When you come to be better acquainted with my daughter, you won't be apt to place so much confidence in her as you do now. I admit I am somewhat of a gambler in the game of life, but if my child can't give me points, and then beat me, my name is not Jim Shannon, and I think it is. Why, do you know, Teddy, that last night, when the soldiers chased John Driscoll to my grounds, I'd have been willing to bet any amount of money that Nell knew just where he was concealed.

TED. Would she dare do such a thing?

SQU. Would she? Well I guess she would. My sweet child would do anything for the man she loves. She resembles her respected parent in that line too much.

TED. She loves him, thin?

SQU. Of course she does. And, come to think of it, I don't blame her a bit, either. He's a dashing sort of a devil-may-care man, just the kind of a chap to captivate any girl. The only objection I have against him is he is Irish. Had he been an Englishman, I'd get a pardon for him and let him marry her.

TED. Thin ye don't like the Irish, sor?

SQU. (*savagely*). No curse it! I hate them all.

TED. An' still ye'd marry Aline, sor. An' ye know she's an Irish girl, an' proud of it.

SQU. (*sharply*). Teddy, that is a different matter altogether. You are now on delicate ground, so be careful where you step.

TED. (*humbly*). I beg yer pardon, sor.

SQU. Granted. But don't refer to it again. Has Captain Gordon been around?

TED. He just lift, sor.

SQU. Humph! I thought so. Seems to me he's making himself mighty free around these premises. I'd like to wring his neck for him, if I dared. The first thing I'll know, he'll be getting a pardon for John Driscoll, and then my work is all undone.

TED. Shure, he just lift to go to Dublin an' get one for him an' his men.

SQU. (*in astonishment*). What! Then the game is up. He'll be back in an hour with the pardon. An hour! My only hope is to capture the prisoner. Once in my power, and nothing can save him. Being an escaped prisoner he will be shot at once — unless Aline promises to become my wife. (*Goes to gate*, C.) While I am gone, Teddy, keep a sharp lookout.

TED. Where are ye going, squire?

SQU. To bring the soldiers here, and station them around the premises, so that they can pounce on Driscoll the moment he makes his appearance. (*Exit, road* R. 3 E.)

TED. (*looking after him*). Ye are a good man Squire Shannon, but I think ye've met yer match at last in the rebel leader, Captain Jack. (*Exit*, R. 3 E.)

(*Enter* NELLIE *from road*, L.)

NEL. (*looking around*). I wonder if John is here yet? He promised to meet me here this morning. (*Anxiously*.) What if he should disappoint me? (*Joyfully*.) Ah, no! He is coming now.

(*Enter* JOHN *from road*, L.)

JOHN. Have I kept you waiting, Nellie? I narrowly escaped being captured again. But here I am at last safe and sound.

NEL. O John, I was afraid you wouldn't come.

JOHN. Trust me, Nellie, to always keep my promise to you. I was making arrangements for leaving Ireland. You know I am a hunted outlaw with a price on my head. Every hand is against me, so what am I to do?

NEL. And must you then leave the home that has sheltered you so long?

JOHN. I must. In some foreign country I can find a home and happiness, which is denied me here.

NEL. But you may receive a pardon.

JOHN. I have no influential friends to plead my case.

NEL. And you are still determined to go?

JOHN. I am. No rest for me in Ireland. And, Nellie dear, you say you love me?

NEL. O John, do you doubt my word?

JOHN. Not I, sweet one. But there are obstacles in the way of our marriage.

NEL. No, John : you are wrong. I know what you would say. But there is no need to, for where you go, I go also.

JOHN. You forget, Nellie, you have a father and a home (*sadly*) ; while, as my wife, you will have no home that you can claim as your own on the face of the earth.

NEL. I care not. I would sacrifice home, wealth, parents, and everything for the man I love. The trials and crosses of your life I will gladly share with you.

JOHN (*clasping her in his arms*). Nellie, you are a woman amongst women. (*Kissing her ; both converse in low tones.*)

(*Enter* TEDDY, R. 3 E.)

TED. (*seeing* NELLIE *and* JOHN). Ah, he is here at last ! And the squire's daughter is with him. An' only to think in a short time he will be behind the bars again. I feel sorry for ye, me poor boy, but shure I can't cry. I wonder is the squire in sight yet? (*Looks off* R. 4 E.) Ah, luck favors the good. He's comin' now. (*Waves his hand to* SQUIRE.)

(*Enter* SQUIRE, R. 4 E.)

SQU. He is here, then?

TED. (*in a whisper*). Shure, he just came, sor.

SQU. And who is the young woman with him? Aline? (*Then in amazement.*) Great Jupiter ! My daughter Nellie !

TED. (*in a whisper*). Spake easy, sor, or they might hear ye.

SQU. How long has she been here?

TED. She just came, sor.

SQU. Hum ! Who arrived first?

TED. Yer daughter, sor.

SQU. Hum ! I thought so. Came here to meet him by appointment, I'll bet. This is a nice affair, I must say. The daughter of Squire Shannon in love with the rebel, Captain Jack. (*Savagely.*) But I'll put an end to all of this. (*Walks slowly to* R. 4 E.)

TED. Where are ye goin' now, squire?

SQU. To hunt up the soldiers. They are less than half a mile from here. (*Shakes fist at* JOHN.) John Driscoll, you will soon be in my power again. (*Exit*, R. 4 E.)

TED. I think I'll be movin' too. (*Exit*, R. 3 E.)

JOHN (*looking at house*, R.). Aline should be up by this time. How still everything is ! No signs of Barney or Kate anywhere.

NEL. (*looking around*). The place seems to be deserted.

JOHN. Something is the matter, sure. (*Looks off* L. 4 E.) Some one is coming now. (*Joyfully.*) And it's Aline.

(*Enter* ALINE, L. 4 E.)

AL. (*seeing her brother*). O John ! (*Runs and kisses him.*) Why do you come here? Look at the risk you run. You will be taken again, and then shot like a dog. (*In surprise to* NELLIE.) And you here too, Miss Shannon?

JOHN (*taking* NELLIE *by the hand*). Aline, this is to be your new sister.

AL. (*in surprise*). What do you mean, John?

JOHN. It means that Nellie has promised to become the future Mrs. John Driscoll.

AL. (*joyfully*). Oh, I am so glad to hear it!

NEL. (*placing arm around* ALINE'S *neck and kissing her*). I am sure, Aline. I shall love you very dearly.

AL. Thank you, dear. And do you know that John is one of the best brothers a sister ever had?

JOHN (*laughing*). That will do for the present, Aline.

AL. Well, you know I speak the truth, John.

NEL. (*laughing*). Aline, the good never like to hear themselves praised. But I fully agree with you as to your brother John being one of the best men in the world.

JOHN (*laughing*). Tush! tush! That is but the opinion of you two.

NEL. Well, we're right. Are we not, Aline?

AL. Of course we are.

(*Enter* BARNEY, L. 4 E.)

BAR. (*out of breath*). Run, masther dear, an' save yourself.

JOHN. What do you mean, Barney?

BAR. Ye have been betrayed again. The soldiers are comin' here to arrest ye.

JOHN. Indeed! Then I had better leave while there is yet time.

AL. (*wildly*). O John, save yourself!

NEL. (*in despair*). Too late. The soldiers are here.

(*Enter soldiers; two stand on each side of gate;* LIEUTENANT, *followed by* SQUIRE, *enter gate,* C.)

SQU. (*pointing to* JOHN). Lieutenant, there stands the rebel who escaped last night.

LIEU. (*placing hand on* JOHN'S *shoulder*). Is your name John Driscoll?

JOHN (*proudly*). Yes: and I have never yet committed a deed that would cause me to hide my face in shame from my fellow-men.

LIEU. That may be all very true; but my duty here is not to bandy words with you, but to arrest you.

SQU. (*sternly*). Lieutenant, do your duty!

LIEU. Come, sir, you are my prisoner.

AL. (*falling on her knees before the* SQUIRE). Squire Shannon, be merciful.

SQU. (*savagely*). Lieutenant, away with him!

LIEU. (*dragging* JOHN *by the arm*). Come, prisoner.

(*Enter* CAPTAIN, *running from* R. 4 E.)

CAP. (*holding up paper*). Hold on, Lieutenant Rogers! I have that man's pardon.

LIEU. Let me see it. (CAPTAIN *hands document to the* LIEUTENANT, *who reads it*.)

CAP. Is everything correct, lieutenant?

LIEU. (*bowing*). Yes, Mr. Gordon.

SQU. (*aside*). Foiled again. (*To* NELLIE.) Come, Nellie; this is no place for you.

NEL. (*proudly*). My place, sir, is by the side of my future husband.

SQU. What is that you say? Do I hear aright?

NEL. You do, sir. I have promised to become the wife of John Driscoll.

JOHN. Your daughter speaks the truth, squire. All we need now is your consent to make us happy.

SQU. (*not heeding him*). Beaten at all points. I played a desperate game and lost. But the stakes were worth trying for. (*To* ALINE.) But it was all done for the love of you, Aline. Will you forgive me?

AL. With all my heart.

JOHN (*to* SQUIRE). Well, sir, I await your answer.

SQU. Answer to what?

JOHN. Whether I get your consent to marry Nellie.

SQU. And if you don't, what then?

JOHN. Well, that's another subject altogether. Don't keep us in suspense. (*Laughing*.) Do you consent?

SQU. Oh, go to the devil! (*To* LIEUTENANT.) Come, lieutenant, we've no business here. (*Exit* SQUIRE *and soldiers, by road,* R.)

BAR. (*holding* TEDDY *by the neck*). An' what will we do with our esteemed friend Mr. Burke here?

JOHN. Let him go. He has done no real harm after all.

BAR. (*releasing him*). Be off with ye.

TED. Shure, it's the good-hearted boy ye are intirely, Barney Donovan. (*Exit*, R. 4 E.)

JOHN. And now all our troubles are at an end. I have won the girl I love; and what more could a young man want than a charming girl like Nellie for a wife?

BAR. (*taking* KATE *by the hand*). An' while yer all gettin' married, I believe I'll try some matrimonial trouble — I mean experience, meself.

ALL. You, Barney?

BAR. Well, of course. Kate has promised to become me own true wife. (*To* KATE.) Haven't ye taken me for betther or worse, darlin'?

KATE. Shure, ye know I have, Barney.

JOHN. Both of you have my consent and blessing. You have been faithful servants in my family, and deserve to be happy. (*To* CAPTAIN.) And, Edward, I know you love my sister Aline. Take her, my boy, and be happy, for you have proved yourself a noble friend.

AL. (*kissing* JOHN). O John, you are an angel!

JOHN (*laughing*). Without wings. But, Aline, you must save your kisses in future for the captain.

CAP. Thank you, John, is all I can say in return. (*Taking* ALINE'S *hand.*) I came to Ireland to hunt rebels; but instead I found my sweet Aline asthore. (*Slow curtain and soft music.*)

POSITION OF CHARACTERS.

BARNEY *and* KATE *at gate*, C.

CAPTAIN *and* ALINE.   JOHN *and* NELLIE.

www.ingramcontent.com/pod-product-compliance
Lightning Source LLC
Chambersburg PA
CBHW061237260626
47172CB00003B/900